EGMONT

We bring stories to life

First published in Great Britain 2011
by Egmont UK Limited,
The Yellow Building, 1 Nicholas Road, London W11 4AN
This edition published in 2015

© 2015 Prism Art & Design Limited.
Based on an original idea by D. Gingell, D. Jones and original
characters created by R. J. M. Lee. All rights reserved.

© 2015 HIT Entertainment Limited.

HIT entertainment

ISBN 978 1 4052 7954 3
48708/9
Printed in Italy

It was Christmas time in Pontypandy.

At the Fire Station, Fireman Sam and Elvis were busy hanging decorations.

Outside, Penny was nearly blown over!

"Woah, it's very windy!" she said, as she rushed across the car park to the Fire Station.

A gust of wind followed Penny inside.

"Oh no!" cried Sam. The tinsel he had just put above the door blew off ... and landed on Station Officer Steele's head!

"Oh, I say!" said Station Officer Steele.

In the kitchen, Elvis was hanging some fairy lights.

"Ta-da! What do you think, Sam?" he asked.

"They look great!" Sam replied.

Elvis went to plug the kettle into the same adaptor as the lights, but Fireman Sam called, "Elvis! Stop!"

"Great Balls of Fire!" cried Elvis. "What's wrong?"

"Putting lots of plugs into one socket can be very dangerous," Sam warned.

He unplugged everything and held up the adaptor. "These can overheat and cause a fire," he said.

Meanwhile, across town, Norman was determined to make the supermarket's Christmas lights the best in Pontypandy.

"Come on, Mum," he said to Dilys, "just one more set, please?"

Dilys was unsure. "We have plenty of lights up already, Norman," she told him. "And besides, I don't have enough sockets to plug them all in safely."

Norman kept pestering, so Dilys plugged an extra set of fairy lights into an adaptor already filled with plugs.

"Let's put this giant Santa balloon on the chimney, too!" said Norman, pulling a box off the shelf.

"Oh, Norman!" said Dilys. "We have enough decorations!"

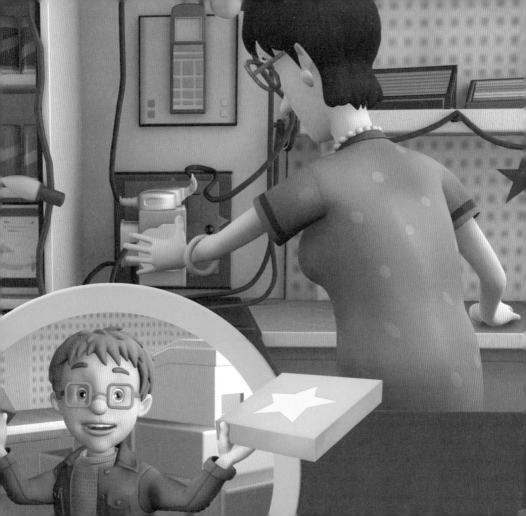

Yet again, Naughty Norman got his own way. Five minutes later, Dilys was halfway up a ladder, holding the giant Santa.

"It's very windy, Norman!" cried Dilys. She tried to climb higher but the ladder wobbled and Santa blew out of her hand!

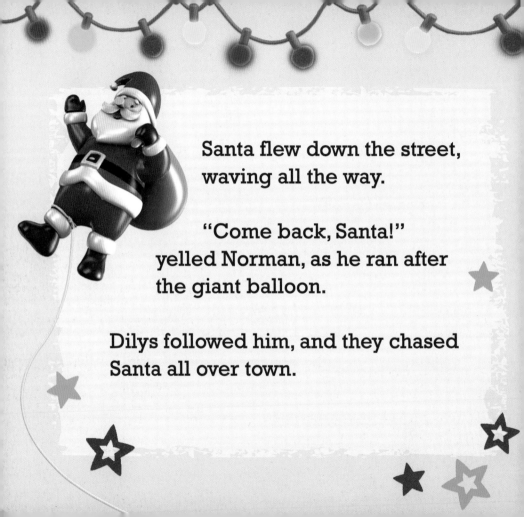

Santa flew down the street,
waving all the way.

"Come back, Santa!"
yelled Norman, as he ran after
the giant balloon.

Dilys followed him, and they chased
Santa all over town.

As Santa blew out of a side street, Norman jumped up to catch the string.

But Santa flew off the end of the Pontypandy docks and out to sea!

"We've lost him," panted Norman. He sighed, and walked back to the shop with Dilys.

Norman was still moaning about losing Santa when Dilys opened the door to the shop ... and screamed as black smoke came pouring out!

"Help! There's a fire! Call Fireman Sam!" she cried.

Norman ran off to call 999.

Station Officer Steele raised the alert.

"Action Stations! Fire at the Cut Price Supermarket!" he called.

Fireman Sam and Elvis slid down the fire pole. Then they sped off in Jupiter, with sirens wailing and lights flashing.

Inside the shop, Fireman Sam saw sparks coming from the overloaded plug adaptor.

"Cut the power!" he called to Elvis.

Elvis ran to the fuse box and threw the switch. "It's off, Sam!"

Sam aimed his powder extinguisher at the plug and fired. WHOOSH!

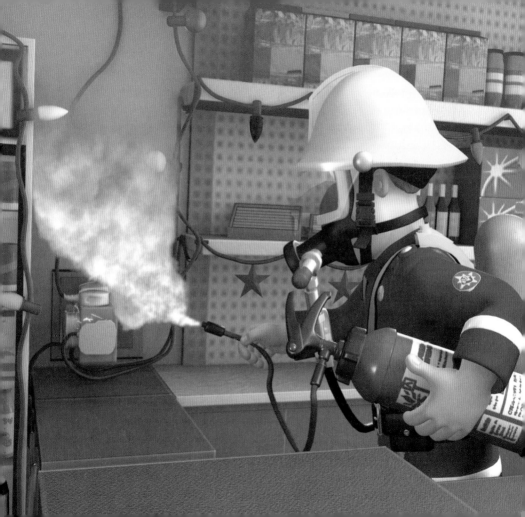

Elvis held up the burnt plug adaptor. "This overheated and caught fire!"

Dilys looked sheepish. "I was going to check it was safe, but then Santa blew away, didn't he, Norman?"

"Sorry," said Norman. "I wanted to have the best decorations in town. But now I'm just glad we can have Christmas at home, thanks to Fireman Sam!"

>→ >→ → The End >→ >→ >→